3 —

Solomon Starbucks Striper

With best wishes -

Ray Rocca

Also by Roy Rowan

Surfcaster's Quest (The Lyons Press)

First Dogs: American Presidents and Their Best Friends
(Algonquin)

Powerful People (Carroll & Graf)

The Intuitive Manager (Little, Brown)

The Four Days of Mayaguez (W. W. Norton)

A Day in the Life of Italy, co-editor (HarperCollins)

Solomon Starbucks Striper

A Fish Story About
Following Your Dreams

Roy Rowan

Illustrations by
Jane Grant Tentas

Book Nook Press

For William

"Man is a rope stretched between
the animal and the Superman—
a rope over an abyss."

Frederick Wilhelm Nietzsche,
Thus Spake Zarathustra

"Men cannot become fish, nor can fish
transform themselves into men. But
over the centuries men have learned to
appreciate in creatures, qualities that
are also recognizable in humans."

John N. Cole,
Striper

"There is a close resemblance between
man and fish in style of exotic grace
of their movements of restrained passion."

Konrad L. Lorenz,
King Solomon's Ring

Prologue

I t is from God that you have received being, life, motion, and sense," preached Saint Anthony of Padua in his Sermon to the Fishes eight hundred years ago. "It is He who has given you your whole world of waters for your habitation. It is He who has furnished it with lodgings, chambers, caverns, grottoes, and such magnificent retirements as are not to be found in the throne rooms of kings, or in the palaces of princes."

As he spoke, the fish came swimming toward him in great multitudes, both from the sea and from the rivers. They quickly arranged themselves, he claimed, according to their species into a beautiful congregation.

"You have the water for your dwelling," Saint Anthony continued, "a clear transparent element, brighter than crystal. You can see from its deepest bottom everything that passes on its surface. You have the eyes of a lynx, or of an Argus. You are guided by a secret and unerring principle, delighting in everything that may be beneficial to you, and avoiding everything that may be harmful.

1

You are carried on by a hidden instinct to preserve yourselves and to propagate your species."

Nowhere today is the propagation process of fish more dramatic than is carried on by striped bass in the spawning grounds of the Nanticoke River, one of twenty-one tributaries feeding Chesapeake Bay. Under the pale spring moon, thousands of lumbering males and females bump heads in nightlong mating dances, leaving billions of fertilized eggs drifting over the pebbly river bottom.

Then as the depleted parents swim away, the single cell within each egg divides. In a day there is already the promise of a tail, and soon after at the other end of the tiny body forming inside the egg's chorion, two dark eyes.

After three or four days the miniature thrashing tail ruptures the membrane, and the fry swims away but with a small sac of nutrients still attached to its abdomen. Within a week, after all the nutrients have been absorbed, the sac disappears and the fry is free. But by then, ninety-nine out of a hundred of its brothers and sisters are dead.

As far as is known, since the species' violent genesis eons ago, just one of the quarter-inch-long survivors was born different from the millions of others. Perhaps it was altered genetically by an electrical charge in the water, caused when a lightning bolt, hurtling down from the heavens, struck a channel marker in the river.

In any case, this particular male fry was stronger, bursting from his egg with a more powerful flick of his tail. His heart was stouter and he was smarter, heading quickly and openmouthed for the shallows along the shore where there was an abundance of plankton on which to feed. Above all, he was stubbornly independent.

The blessed Father Saint Anthony would surely have told this unusual newborn striper, as he was wont to say to all of the revered fish in his congregation, "In you are seen the mighty mystery of an infinite goodness." And indeed, this striper was ordained to be good.

More mysteriously, he was destined as a magnificent mature striper to develop powers of perception never before bestowed on a fish. Or was it simply that he, like the fisherman who forever fantasizes about catching such a beauty, would become an incurable dreamer?

"I was relegated to a position in the rear."

One

Solomon Starbucks Striper is my name. Why such a fancy name for a fish? you might wonder, even though anglers and Epicureans alike consider striped bass among the most prized denizens of the sea.

Well, the name wasn't really my doing. My schoolmates are to blame. One day, a young friend swam up through the shafts of golden light slicing into the sea and called out, "Hey, Solomon Starbucks Striper, what'd you learn in school today?"

My friend was a wise guy, always kidding around, like yelling, "SHARK!" when a toothless dogfish wandered by. And he knew I hated school, or he wouldn't have baited me with that silly question.

"Whom do you think you're talking to?" I replied with false indignation, playing along with his game.

"You," he said. "We decided to call you Solomon, because you're so piscinely serious."

That was true. Ever since my small-fry days in Chesapeake Bay I was indeed serious, eager to learn about the tides, undertows, and other mysteries of the ocean.

5

"But what about the *Starbucks*?" I asked. "That's a ridiculous middle name."

Then my friend turned serious. Tactfully as possible, he told me that although I couldn't see my own stripes, because of some strange genetic defect mine were coffee-colored, not black like the stripes on the rest of our species.

I was stunned. Nobody had ever hinted at this before. But it did explain why some of the more color-conscious stripers had been swimming clear of me in school. And why on long migratory journeys I was relegated to a position in the rear—way back where another member of the school was forced to swim in disgrace after being caught, tagged, and released.

But he had only his own greed to blame—always pushing and shoving at mealtime, until one morning in a gluttonous lunge he snapped at a piece of blue and white plastic with hooks on it. We all watched gleefully as he zigged and zagged crazily through the foaming surf and finally disappeared up on the beach. When he reappeared, a yellow tag was pinned behind his dorsal fin, noting the date and place of his humiliating mistake.

My case, I felt, was entirely different, having done nothing wrong except to be blessed, if you could call it that, with the wrong colored stripes imprinted on my shiny silver scales.

"Aren't we fish supposed to be color-blind?" I blurted to my friend in self-defense, although I knew we're not.

My friend seemed embarrassed, too, and quickly sought to make me feel better. "Starbucks has a strong masculine sound,"

6

he said. "Anyway, it's a lot better than Morone saxatilis, the Latin name the ichthyologists stuck us striped bass with."

I couldn't disagree with that. Especially since those same ichthyologists had also labeled us anadromous, indicating that we are some sort of odd fish, comfortable in either fresh water or salt water.

For a while the news made me very self-conscious. I felt imprisoned by the seven coffee-colored stripes, running from gill to tail, down each side. Especially after our fat, old schoolmaster swam up and said, "It's too bad, Solomon, but you just don't blend in. Better try another school."

Several times I sidled up to a sailboat riding at anchor to study my reflection in its shiny fiberglass hull. Either the water was too murky, or the hull's surface wasn't glossy enough to catch the color of my stripes.

The next year I switched schools and dropped my middle name. Surprisingly, my new schoolmates didn't pick on my stripes, though deep inside I still bore the shame. But they did ridicule the idea of my being called Solomon.

"That name might be suitable for a wise old bull bass," they jeered. "But not for a young buck who doesn't know his anal fin from his dorsal. From now on we're going to call you Solo for short."

That was fine with me. Solo had a nice lilt to it, reminiscent of the songs we sometimes heard whales and dolphins singing. Besides, Solo expressed my growing urge to quit school and go

7

it alone. I was tired of being a groupie—not a grouper, mind you—with several hundred of us schoolies swimming nose-to-tail like links in a long silver chain.

Traveling north from Chesapeake Bay, our schoolmaster would lead us close by Atlantic City, not a rewarding place for healthy appetites. The garish casino lights, designed to attract gamblers, turned the ocean a lurid yellow, green, and purple, scaring all the herring away. We'd leave there with our stomachs as empty as the pockets of the invading army of slot machine addicts.

Sandy Hook, however, our next landfall, was a feasting place, teeming with herring, sand eels, and an occasional croaker. Gliding into the curve of a cresting wave, we'd drive the disoriented baitfish straight into our open mouths, filling our guts until they were ready to burst.

Then on under the Verrazano Bridge we would swim, and into the polluted waters of New York Harbor, so filled with sludge it was hard to see. After dodging all the tugs and barges, we finally entered Long Island Sound.

A boring journey? You bet! Even after reaching the blue Atlantic, our schoolmaster never let us out of the sight of land for fear of running into a yellowfin tuna or great white shark.

Stripers, we were told, aren't built to venture more than two or three miles offshore. It was another one of those self-imposed physical limitations drummed into us in school.

"Don't worry if you accidentally wash up onto the beach,"

8

our schoolmaster assured us. "Keep calm, and the next wave will carry you back out." But not without certain hazards, I discovered.

Once, after riding a monster rogue wave, I was lying on my side in the shallows with my right eye buried in the sand. When I opened my left eye and looked up, there stood a fisherman, rod in hand, peering down at me in utter amazement.

"I'll be goddamned," I heard him swear before the next wave swept me safely out again. "I've been trying to catch one of you bastards all morning." If his reflexes had been a little quicker, he could have reached down and grabbed me by the tail.

Every spring we'd swim as far north as Cape Cod, then quickly return to our protected home waters in the Chesapeake as soon as the ocean chilled. "Safety in numbers" was the basic lesson beaten into what the schoolmaster kept referring to as our "thick fish heads." But I sensed that playing it safe was one of life's most foolish rules.

Regimented living might be all right for mackerel or menhaden, who must close ranks to protect themselves from marauding blues. Or even from the likes of us when we're in a feeding frenzy. But for a strong young striper, bursting with energy and curiosity, school was dull enough to make my tail go limp, to say nothing of my brain.

We were all forced to frolic in the same surf, dine on the same easily obtained fast food, mainly silversides and sand eels. And when it came time to spawn, we males were supposed to spread our sperm—or "milt" according to the ichthyologists—

indiscriminately over any eggs in the vicinity. It didn't matter whether or not we caught the eye or spotted the shapely tail of an attractive female.

Our close communal living, nevertheless, was not risk- free. If a red tide, or some other poisonous bacteria, infected the waters, thousands of us were likely to find ourselves belly-up on the beach. Or if the outstretched nets of a trawler happened by, hundreds more of us might be scooped up and perish in one pass. The prospect of all of us living and dying together was taking all the fun out of being a striper.

Most everywhere we went seemed to be dictated by our voracious appetites or by fear. As a result, we never ventured out to the nearby islands of Cuttyhunk, Nantucket, or Martha's Vineyard, known for their dramatic shorelines. Block Island, famous for its shipwrecks that all fish love to explore, was off-limits too.

Other schools traveled all the way up to Nova Scotia, where they enjoyed superb underwater sight-seeing, plus an abundance of savory scallops. We never made it up to the rockbound coast of Maine.

Even worse, we weren't inspired to improve ourselves, nor challenged to achieve new personal goals. Our leaders, for example, never encouraged us to try soaring leaps like a tarpon, or to streak bullet-fast through the shallows like a bonito, or even to play hide-and-seek among the rocks like a blackfish. Let's face it: Our leaders were as lazy as sea slugs, interested in little else but filling their own stomachs and staying out of the stomachs of others. "Isn't there more to life?" I often asked them?

Only Sam Socrates Striper, the worldliest bass in our school, ever alluded to the wonders of the deep that were there to explore. But old "Soc," as we called him, was a cold fish, too closemouthed to talk about his escapades.

"On your travels, what truths did you learn?" I once asked him.

"The truth is always strange," he replied with his usual reticence. "You will surely find that is true." His answer made my frustrations even worse, although they'd been growing gradually, and mainly at night when we weren't on the move.

So while my schoolmates were either chasing baitfish on the surface or, with their bellies full, slumbering peacefully on the bottom, I began wandering off on short, exhilarating swims into neighboring bays and harbors.

Some nights I'd explore the barnacle-encrusted boats at anchor, or chase some skinny squid between the piles of a dock. Other nights I'd make practice swirls on the smooth, moonlit surface in earshot of the noisy night herons squawking on the shore.

By dawn I would always rejoin the school. "Watch out, Solo!" my friends warned me. "Keep wandering off and you'll be eaten alive." But then my schoolmates had sharp tongues and were always wisecracking. So I quoted back to them the old proverb "Fish die because they open their mouths."

11

I wasn't scared of dying. Instead, I felt an overpowering exuberance for life, an irrepressible dream to swim in new waters and face new challenges. The lingering stigma of my stripes, I suppose, was also goading me on. But more than anything, I hungered for adventure.

One night after swimming in and out of several bays, I just kept going. I said to myself, "Solomon Starbucks Striper, or Solo as they call you, from now on you're going to live up to your nickname and strike out on your own."

Sucking extra oxygen from the water flowing through my gills, and flexing the muscles in my broad, powerful tail, I headed out to sea.

"I ran headlong into a tangle of seaweed."

Two

Happily skipping from one wave to another, I glimpsed the fading stars and ghostly glow of last night's moon. The sea was still ominously dark, except for the white, windblown spray whipping off the wave tops.

At first being alone felt strange, and I must admit a bit alarming. No schoolmates darting in and around me. Nobody to talk to. No one else deciding which way to swim in search of breakfast, though I was still too exhilarated by my newfound freedom to feel hungry. Nobody around even to make fun of the coffee-colored stripes running down my sides.

"Solo," I said, "you'll just have to get used to talking to yourself—and listening to the voice of the sea."

Not that the ocean is a great conversationalist. It's easy to tell from when it's angry, from its deep-throated roar. Or when it's friendly, from the soft lapping sound it makes gently hitting against the shore. Other times the ocean is unfathomable.

"In any case, Solo," I decided, "you better listen carefully to

15

what little the ocean has to say. For too many years you've been relying on your schoolmaster to sound the warning of an impending storm or tidal surge."

In school, you see, the emphasis was on networking—considered essential for both getting ahead and eluding trouble. Say we were seeking a trove of tiny shrimp in a sunken ship, or stopping one of our schoolmates from snapping at a temptingly baited hook, we networked. We didn't call it that, because we avoided using any word with net in it. But the fact is, we relied too much on each other. And we never tested ourselves.

Now alone, skipping carefree from wave to wave, I was determined to teach myself how to jump—something I'd always dreamed of doing because it enables a fish to see far ahead. "How pitiful," I thought. "Ranked among the top game fish in the sea, and we can't even jump."

Couldn't be a physical problem, because stripers are strong. We're not a bunch of weakfish. And it's not due to a lack of determination, because we aren't jellyfish either. Must be mainly a matter of practice—an important part of our training that the senior stripers in our school neglected. Or perhaps those fifty- and sixty-pound lunkers were just too fat.

"Practice," I said to myself. "That's it!"

After all, practice at a young age made us feel at home in the most violent places where the sea and land came together. Trial and error taught us how to race through the arc of a breaking wave, swirl in the rolling surf, and somersault in a turbulent

16

riptide. Using the strength in our broad shoulders and powerful tail, we mastered all those forces of the sea like no other fish had. Those were the skills expected of a striper.

With practice, I felt sure, I could also learn how to flick my tail, arch my torso, and leap into the air like a bluefish. Or, better yet, soar like a tarpon, though I've heard of overzealous tarpon jumping right into the boats of the fishermen trying to catch them—a shortcut, for sure, to the taxidermist's shop. And who wants to spend years hanging, stuffed to the gills, on the wall of some smoke-filled tavern, listening to the barflies regaling each other with fish stories?

To find a good place to practice jumping, I headed in toward shore. The sun's fireball was just climbing over the horizon, setting the ocean ablaze. Watching deep-blue water turn fiery red at dawn is one of the most amazing sights a fish ever sees.

But at sunrise there are too many shark fins ominously cutting the surface to risk swimming on top. Of course, for a great white, mako, or tiger shark, a striper would be no more than a snack.

So, for safety' sake, I swam along the bottom, far below the red-tinted waves. Whole armies of fiddler crabs scurried out of my way. Ordinarily, I might have paused for a little light refreshment. But I ignored them, along with the other crustaceans.

As the water grew shallower, it also became warmer, and I could see rays of bright sunlight once again filtering down from above.

The depth, I figured, was about thirty feet, slightly more than ten times my own length. And the sea's surface was almost flat, rippled just a little by an offshore breeze. Perfect conditions, I decided, to practice jumping.

"No big deal," I thought, gathering courage for my first trial leap. "This is going to be a lead-sinker cinch."

First, I fluttered my fins to get in a vertical position, with my nose pointing straight up, and the tip of my tail barely touching the sandy bottom. Then, closing my mouth, clamping my gill plates shut, and folding down both my front and rear dorsal fins so they lay flat against my back, I turned myself into a streamlined piscine projectile. Over and over I began repeating my new mantra: "Jump! Jump! Jump!"

"Ready for liftoff," I humorously announced, as if a cheering group of spectators might be watching. Slowly, I began to whip my broad tail back and forth, propelling my body up toward the surface.

"Faster! Faster!" I heard myself shout, though with the sinking feeling that I might have to abort. I didn't seem to be gaining enough speed. And I guess I wasn't. Only the front end of my body broke the surface before it and the rest of me splashed back down in an embarrassing bellyflop.

I was glad no other fish were watching. "What a miserable attempt," I thought. "Even young snapper blues jump better than that." I felt like diving down to the bottom and burying my head in the sand.

I could almost hear my former schoolmates jeering: "Solomon Starbucks Striper, you're an embarrassment to us all.

18

Resume your position at the rear of the school."

Suddenly, it hit me: "Stupid striper! You did it bass ackwards, starting at the bottom. You ignored the basic hydrodynamics involved in jumping. No wonder you couldn't pick up sufficient speed. You started your vertical ascent way down where the water pressure is greatest. By the time you reached the surface, your energy was sapped."

Bluefish, I'd noticed, don't do that. They gather speed chasing small fish near the top, before leaping out of the water, usually with their mouths still full of food. But then they're an uncouth, violently gluttonous bunch, without an ounce of sophistication.

Even so, blues seemed to have an instinctive understanding of the hydrodynamics of jumping. I decided to copy their technique, beginning my next practice attempt just a foot or so below the surface.

Once again, I closed my mouth and gills, and collapsed my fins so they lay flat against my scales. Then, whipping my tail back and forth, I shot ahead, rapidly gaining speed. For a moment I thought I couldn't go any faster.

"Solo, you can do it!" I exclaimed, beating my tail even harder.

The water was rushing by so fast that I felt my scales heating up. With one final thrust of my tail, I suddenly veered upward, breaking the surface. For a split second my whole body hung in the air before clumsily crashing.

A couple of cod, who happened to be watching, flapped their

19

fins in mock applause. "Bass can't jump," I heard one of them whisper. "Must be some kind of freak fish with coffee-colored stripes."

"Were those stupid cod prejudiced, or just envious?" I wondered, though I was too eager to try another jump to really care. My heart was beating with excitement. Next time I wanted to hang in the air gracefully for more than a split second, and then slice back cleanly into the water.

Swimming away from the two cod, I readied myself for another practice leap, one that would be my absolute personal best: two whole seconds suspended in the air, before knifing back into the water in an Olympic-perfect dive.

This time I began by remaining almost motionless while hyperventilating like crazy. I wanted to absorb as much dissolved oxygen as possible into my bloodstream. After completing the other preliminaries to make myself streamlined, I threw my tail into gear.

My body shot forward like an arrow, but headlong into a tangle of seaweed.

For a few seconds I was so dazed I didn't hear the two stupid cod guffawing. "Those coffee-colored stripes are driving him crazy," one of them chortled. "He's trying rub them off in the seaweed."

No use getting mad at a couple of dumb cod, a species of bottom-feeders so stupid that they swim around with their mouths wide open, eating whatever washes in. Anyway, the weight of failure was worse than their jeering. So I kept my cool and swam into water too shallow for the cod to follow.

By this time, the sun was high in the sky, and the water was brilliantly clear. Not a wisp of seaweed to be seen. And no kibitzers around to make caustic comments.

On the next attempt all systems were go: gills clamped shut, fins flat against my body, and my tail generating tremendous thrust as I shot up and burst out of the sea.

Suddenly, there I was, Superstriper, soaring through the air like a bird. An entirely new sensation. Not swimming, but flying, the soft wind whispering in my face.

And taking wing for a fleeting moment, I looked down on a brilliant aquatic world I had viewed only myopically from below. Never before had I even dreamed of the ocean's vastness: waves, marching off majestically one after another, almost forever it appeared, until they met the sky.

"Where in the world did those waves come from?" I wondered. "And where are they going?" Those two questions triggered several others.

"Does this world end and another begin where the sky falls into the sea?

"Could a mere striper swim there?

"And if so, what would he discover? A world of fresh ideas and unlimited opportunities? Even for a social outcast like me?"

Echoing in my head, I kept hearing the words of sage old Sam Socrates Striper: "The truth is always strange. You will surely find that is true."

Knifing back into water, I vowed to find the answers, strange or not.

"Solo," I said, "you've learned how to jump. For a striper, that's quite an achievement. But it's only a stunt. Not a very inspiring goal for a true adventurer.

"Now you have an important new goal. One that could finally break the psychological chains that hold back all stripers from reaching their true potential.

"So swim on! Swim fast! Swim far! Until you reach that place where the sky falls into the sea. And the new world beyond."

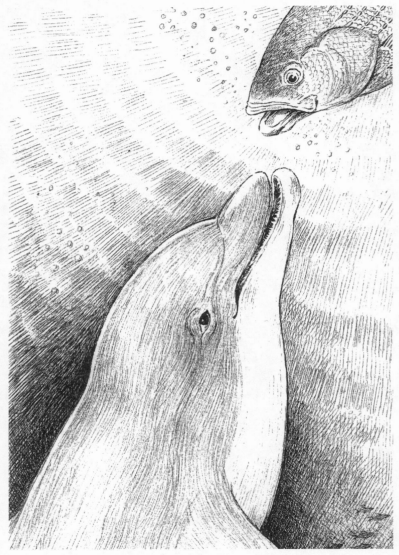

"Glancing back, I saw the bottle-nose of a porpoise."

Three

W hat a strange yet exhilarating sensation, swimming so far from shore in water so deep I couldn't see bottom. No sandbars, no rocks, no submerged signposts of any kind to guide me. Nothing to navigate with but my own internal compass.

The horizon was tinged with red. Suddenly the sun appeared straight ahead, confirming that I was on course.

"Solo, your compass is infallible," I kept reassuring myself. "Remember, we stripers have confounded fishermen forever by the way we swim up and down the Atlantic Coast—sometimes thousands of miles—and still find our way home."

Most marine scientists claim we are guided by the gravitational attraction of the sun and moon. Or perhaps by celestial signals unknown to man. Others say it's our acute sense of smell. Still, I felt a little nervous swimming alone so far out to sea, away from the coast.

"Solo," I said, "where's your backbone? That compass of yours has been safely guiding stripers ever since the Ice Age.

Didn't one of your most distant forebears, a veritable Moses, lead our species down through the great freshwater channels gouged by the glaciers, all the way from Labrador to the Atlantic? And with nothing but his own compass to go by."

I knew all that. Nevertheless, we modern-day stripers are accustomed to leaving the navigational duties to our schoolmaster. Or occasionally to the schoolmistress, although the male chauvinists in school claimed that female stripers suffer from an inferior sense of direction.

"She'd get lost in a bathtub" was the kind of snide grumbling you'd hear when the schoolmistress took over. But as I've said before, prejudice frequently reared its ugly head, or I wouldn't have been ostracized for being born with the wrong- colored stripes.

Actually, I wasn't born with them. At birth, all of us stripers are white as freshwater perch from whom we were descended. After about only six months, as we enter adolescence, do our black lateral stripes appear. Except mine, of course, which like an underexposed photograph came out the color of coffee.

Fishermen rarely see us unstriped—in our birthday suits, so to speak. We hide in the rivers and bays until we're three or four years old. Finally we schoolies venture out into the Atlantic. But always with a senior striper leading the way.

Thinking back about those formative years, I still resented being treated as an outcast, forced to swim "shotgun"—really "shark bait"—at the tail end of the school. On the other hand, being segregated helped prepare me for the lonesome journey I'm on.

I was finding that swimming alone had some unexpected advantages. Nobody to bump and scrape scales with. Nobody to race for the next mouthful of food. Ichthyologists, who claim to have found everything from seagull feathers to cigarette lighters in our bellies, blame us for being subject to uncontrolled feeding frenzies.

I agree. But were we really put in this world just to eat? Could our existence be so devoid of a real purpose?

As I've said to myself many times, "Surely there must be more to life. A higher purpose than just filling our guts for fifteen, twenty, or even twenty-five years." Provided, of course, we escaped hook, spear, and net for that long a time.

I felt determined to find out what that higher purpose was, as I continued swimming east to where the sky meets the sea.

You see, being alone far out in the Atlantic had put me in contemplative mood. I was also struck by the idea that we stripers are guided by a second internal compass. Not just the celestial one that keeps us swimming on course. But another compass that directs our aspirations, sets our goals, and measures our achievements. Yes, and channels our dreams.

"What else, Solo," I asked myself, "could have prodded you into learning how to jump, an ability that doesn't come naturally to stripers?

"Not that jumping isn't important for survival. Suppose a

party boat were anchored up ahead, full of fishermen tossing baited hooks in your direction. Or worse yet, a shark languishing on the surface in the sun. How else would you know of the danger lurking?"

From a jump into the air, it's easy to tell the triangular fin of a voracious shark from the new-moon crescent of a finicky swordfish—too fussy an eater to munch on us thick-sculled stripers. "Lucky, aren't we," I thought, "that our bony heads can sometimes serve as protective helmets."

Of course, our thick skulls would never discourage even the most dyspeptic shark from gobbling us up. Only rapid acceleration and the agility to dodge and turn have ever kept even the most courageous striper from being instantly ripped to pieces by a shark's razor-sharp teeth. The mere thought of that final moment made my scales stand on end.

"So, Solo, how do you survive a shark attack?" I asked myself, still unnerved by the mental picture of being chewed to pieces. "There must be a way."

Regaining my cool, I began to analyze the problem. Short bursts of speed are a striper's birthright. Stamina and sustained speed are not. But why not? Like jumping, perhaps long-distance speedswimming is mainly a matter of practice.

"Sustained speed! Sustained speed!" became my new mantra as I raced through the ocean.

Several bodybuilding exercises, I realized, had to be worked on as well—like developing more muscles in my tail for added endurance, and strengthening the feathery red filaments in my gills to absorb more energy-giving oxygen from the sea.

"And you better work off that gut!" I heard a voice coming from behind me say. "Your bulging belly's slowing you down."

Glancing back I was startled to see the blue bottle-nose of a female porpoise, her mouth angled upward in a smile.

"You practically scared me to death," I said. "But how'd you know what I was thinking?"

"Telepathy," replied the porpoise, in a high-pitched squeal. "We're pretty good mind readers, you know."

I had seen a porpoise only once before, playfully hop- skipping along in the bow wave of an oil tanker in Long Island Sound. But the only word that porpoise spoke sounded like a sneeze.

"Where are you from?" I asked, still stunned to discover I had company way out in the ocean.

"Spain," she replied, pointing her left flipper at the eastern horizon. "My name is Carmencita Phocoena Phocoena. But you can call me Carmen."

I figured some stuttering ichthyologist must have given her that double-barreled family name. Spain, I also figured, must be an island off Cape Cod, but I didn't want to show my stupidity. "So, what brings you here?" I asked instead.

"To teach you how to swim faster, Senor. I heard you mulling over the problem in your head."

Amazing, the mental powers of porpoises, I thought. Or maybe it's just porpoises from Spain.

"First," she said, settling down to business, "you must learn how to use your pectoral and pelvic fins as power boosters. And shorten your tail strokes. You're wasting too much energy."

Before the lessons ended, she had picked apart just about everything we'd been taught in school. "Most of you stripers," she complained, "don't learn more than the basics of swimming—how to move from reef to reef, or inlet to inlet, in search of one meal after another."

Carmen sure hit the nail on the head. We really are a piggy bunch of fish, more concerned with eating than perfecting new skills.

"The problem's psychological," she added. "You aren't challenged to enhance the powers nature endowed you with."

And before I could say another word, she started reciting all the body mechanics involved in moving faster through the water.

"Once you learn these principles of propulsion," she explained, "you can combine speed swimming with arcing leaps into the air, just the way we do."

I couldn't picture myself hitting twenty-five knots, jumping and diving porpoiselike, all the while trying to keep pace with some super tanker. But telling her that wouldn't have been polite.

I was barely able to express my heartfelt thanks, before Carmen squealed, "Adios amigo," flipped her tapered tail, and sped away.

Trying to forget all my old self-defeating perceptions of

swimming wasn't easy. But after a month of concerted practice, coupled with intensive dieting and arduous training, my endurance vastly improved.

As Carmen promised would happen, I started getting twice the speed with half the effort. It was easy to tell. During the day while it was still light, the sea whipping past my eyes appeared as an indigo blur. And streaking along at night, I could look back and see a glowing phosphorous trail left by my wake—like the fiery tail of a comet. Still, I kept right on practicing until I was a virtual torpedo shooting through the sea.

The ocean floor, I also noticed, kept falling away, indicating that I was speeding back and forth into the deep Atlantic trough called the Canyon. But those were all dry runs, if that term applies to practice sessions in the ocean. And with no predators in hungry pursuit.

"Would all systems still be go," I wondered, "with a real shark on my tail?" I was debating that question when a fluid gray form appeared in the distance, just the shadowy outline of something large and ominous.

Weaving from side to side, its hulking shape was impossible to identify. Yet there was something miraculous in the suddenness of its appearance. The surface of the sea was far above, its absence contributing to the eeriness of the moment.

As the gray form came closer, propelled by sinuous swimming movements, I made out its large pointed snout. And imbedded in the head was a wide black eye—just a black hole with no visible pupil in it. Still there was no threat. No movement of aggression from this unsightly monster.

"Shark! Shark!" I heard a voice screaming inside my head. "Wake up, Solo! It's a shark!"

Transfixed by the wide black eye, I remained motionless, momentarily paralyzed.

Slowly and deliberately the shark moved forward, closing the gap between us. I could now see silky furrows in its skin, revealing a pattern of incredible muscles extending from the back of its head all the way to its tail. And when its huge maw opened, the rippling muscles in its throat also came into play.

Each time I tried backing away, the shark came closer, its ferocious mouth forming into the grin of a passionless killer. Or was that grin simply a sign of amusement at my coffee-colored stripes?

For a moment I was confused, my fear suddenly mixed with feelings of admiration.

"Really a superbly beautiful animal," I had to admit. "Not an evil-looking creature, except for its mouth. After prowling the seas since prehistoric days, isn't this big fish, like the rest of us, just trying to survive?"

The shark was close enough to perceive the slightest pressure wave from my smallest movement. Then, in a sudden change of mood, its eyes rolled white, the sign of attack. And without further warning, it began circling menacingly around me.

The circles became inexorably smaller, leaving little room for me to back off. I can't remember precisely what happened next.

Except that propelled by stark fear and a tremendous burst of energy, I shot ahead, right past the pointed snout and wide-open mouth.

Never pausing to dodge, turn, or look back, and without a moment wasted on any more thoughts of what it would feel like clamped between those mighty jaws, I headed northeast in the direction of Nantucket.

As I sped through the water, my fears fell away, replaced by the fierce concentration it took to outrace my pursuer.

My only worry then was that other sharks, drawn by invisible signals from the one chasing me, would suddenly appear from the open sea and intercept my escape. Fortunately, none did.

"Solo," I said to myself, trembling with delight on the ocean floor. "Whatever it was that drove you to practice sustained speed just saved your life."

But I had also learned something else: Keeping my fear under control helped me escape.

I was in such a celebratory mood that I failed to notice what I first dismissed as an apparition: the ghostly carcass of an ocean liner, lying on the bottom, not more than a hundred yards away.

"They don't call me the Old Philoctopus for nothing," he said.

Four

S triped bass don't ever dream of boarding a luxury liner, except perhaps on a silver platter garnished with parsley. So it was with baited (a word we fish hate) breath—or better, unabated curiosity—that I swam through an open porthole of the enormous passenger ship I had accidentally discovered.

Her single smokestack was painted red, white, and green, the colors of the Italian flag. So I asked myself, "Really, could this barnacle-encrusted old tub have once been Italy's glamorous maiden of the seas?"

It was only after circling the seven-hundred-foot-long hull and carefully scrutinizing the corroded letters on her stern, that I could tell this was indeed the Andrea Doria from Genoa, now resting in her ocean grave midway between Block Island and Nantucket.

But then, how glamorous could a liner look after lying on her ruptured right side, under two hundred feet of water for almost half a century?

"A perfect example of the fine line between life and death," I thought.

Here was this magnificent vessel, created by a celebrated marine architect, constructed by the most skilled craftsmen, and decorated by the most imaginative interior designers, only to have her life snatched away by a tiny wrong turn in the fog.

Many of my schoolmates had their lives snatched away after taking a tiny wrong turn into the outstretched net of a dragger. That was understandable. But a huge ocean liner? The mere thought of it gave me chills as I entered the dead hulk.

What I was most curious to see was the ship's gorgeous decor. Divers scavenging for souvenirs reported finding exquisite paintings by Michelangelo, Raphael, and Titian still adorning the walls of the first class lounges.

Fakes, I suppose. But then how many stripers get to see even copies of the great Italian masters?

I said to myself, "Solo, this should be a culturally uplifting experience."

But I also knew it could turn out to be a foolhardy adventure. Several of the divers had run out of air and died exploring the labyrinthine interior. Even a fish, I figured, could get lost and never find the way out.

But you know that old cliché, "The greatest risk is not taking one." As must be obvious by now, ever since leaving school, I've been seeking new adventures and training myself to take more risks. So my curiosity to see what treasures still remained inside this twenty-nine-thousand-ton sunken liner just couldn't be curbed.

An open porthole was the only means of entry I could find. The large gash ripped in the Doria's starboard side by the bow of the Swedish liner Stockholm was now buried under coarse yellow sand. And the hatches were all bolted shut. Anyway, I had already taken a turn around all three outdoor pools looking for another way in.

Once inside, I found myself swimming along a dark passage-way on the upper deck. Fortunately, as nocturnal feeders, we stripers see clearly in the black of night, or at depths where there is no light at all.

Even in the dark everything inside still looked surprisingly shipshape—except between cabins 42 and 58, where the metal was badly mangled and the wood splintered from the impact of the two ships colliding.

"How exciting," I thought, "to actually be aboard one of these floating palaces whose bottoms are all we fish ordinarily see."

Up the main staircase to the promenade deck I swam, into the first class lounge, and then farther forward into the extrava-gantly decorated grand ballroom. "As long as you're aboard, Solo, you might as well go first-class," I kiddingly told myself.

I was reveling in all the waterlogged luxury when suddenly my scales stood on end. Not a shark this time. But there in the middle of the ballroom stood a tall man.

"A drowned passenger? Or one of the dead divers perfectly

preserved by the brine?" were my first ghoulish thoughts. The man gripped a sword in his right hand. His hollow eyes stared menacingly at me as if to say, "Swim no closer or I'll smite you dead!"

"Solo," I said, trying to bolster my courage, "if you can look a live shark in the eye, the cold stare of a human corpse shouldn't scare you."

Swimming closer, I discovered how silly my fears were. The corpse was cast in bronze, and his sword was still in its scabbard, posing no threat at all. A tarnished nameplate on the pedestal under the gentleman's feet revealed that he was the heroic six-teenth-century Italian Admiral Andrea Doria, for whom the unlucky liner was named.

My fears had barely subsided when the statue suddenly began to dance, sending me skittering off into a corner of the ballroom.

"Jumpin' Jonah! Not even the most lifelike sculpture could come alive! Or could it?"

The movement of his two legs was unmistakable. And his left hand, the one not holding the sword, seemed to be waving to me to join in his dance.

"Don't be ridiculous. Stripers can't dance," I felt like saying, when I noticed it wasn't the statue's arm that was waving to me, but a long tentacle protruding from behind.

Darting to one side, I glimpsed the rest of what was the most gruesome looking sea monster I'd ever seen. Its bulbous head had a fierce mouth, armed with a powerful parrotlike beak. Two warty eyes, set close together, emitted a demonic glare.

The bottom part of this creature was even more grotesque. From its lumpy oval body radiated eight writhing arms, reaching out to about five feet in every direction. And lining each of these tentacles were two rows of slimy suction cups, used, I suppose, to clamp onto some unsuspecting prey.

"Ugly!" I said to myself. "I've never seen such an ugly beast!" Yet, to my astonishment, the giant octopus turned out to be not only friendly, but a remarkably wise old geezer as well.

"What brings you to my private preserve?" asked the octopus in deep-throated grunts and growls as repelling as his appearance.

"I didn't mean to trespass on your private preserve," I replied politely. "My curiosity to see the inside of this great ocean liner simply got the best of me."

"But, striper, what are you doing way out here? Why aren't you back in a preppy East Coast school?" the ugly creature asked, his two lidless eyes extending forward on long protuberances to get a closer look at me.

"I'm on a far journey to where the sky meets the sea," I explained.

"Where the sky meets the sea!" echoed the octopus shaking his tentacles. "It does that here! There! Everywhere!"

"What do you mean?" I asked, curious as to whether this denizen of dark crevices had ever glimpsed the sky.

"Silly striper. Wherever you are is where the sky meets the sea," persisted the octopus.

"What a stubborn old cephalopod!" I thought. But I didn't want to be disrespectful, so I told him how every time I jumped, I could actually see, far off in the distance, the sky descending like an azure curtain, right down to the sea.

"That's an optical illusion," railed the octopus gleefully. "You could keep on swimming and jumping forever and never reach this place you are seeking."

My crestfallen look must have been obvious. "If you don't believe me, go ask a barnacle," added the octopus. "Barnacles go round and round the world clinging to the bottoms of tankers and container ships. Yet they never reach the place you are talking about, where the sky meets the sea. As any barnacle will tell you, it's always just beyond the most distant wave."

I still wasn't convinced. But I could see the octopus turning red. Octopi, I knew, can turn many different colors. But red, I assumed, was a sign of his growing impatience.

"And if you could reach this illusory place where the sky meets the sea, what would you expect to find?" he continued grilling (another word we fish hate) me.

"A new and better world," I replied.

"Oh, striper, you are a silly fish," chortled the octopus, squirting a cloud of black ink in my direction, as if that would blot out my illusions. "You can't swim your way into a better world, I'm afraid. Only an altered state of mind can lead you there."

40

Octopi, I'd also heard, are highly intelligent. Still, I was slightly irritated by this one's know-it-all attitude. "And how can you be so sure of that?" I asked.

"They don't call me the Old Philoctopus for nothing," he replied. "Trust me. The secret is to turn your thoughts inward. That way you can let go of your limited striper's-eye view of the world in favor of a greatly expanded one. Only then will you find a better world. One full of opportunities you never envisioned before."

"Sounds like some sort of a mental trick," I said, still unconvinced.

"In a way it is. The trick is to relax your mind so it delves into your subconscious, an area of the brain teeming with creative ideas and ambition."

"But I'm talking about a real place in the ocean, not an imaginary place in my mind," I countered with growing irritation.

"And where may I ask is that?" harrumphed the Old Philoctopus.

"I don't know precisely where, but I understand it's somewhere near Vana."

"You mean Nirvana," roared the octopus, his flabby stomach shaking with laughter. "Nirvana's not a place. It's the blissful state of oblivion where you feel no pain and have no worries."

I was about to interrupt and say, "That's exactly what I'm seeking," when he added, "But Nirvana is unattainable. We philoctopi know that."

41

I was crushed. My disappointment was now complete. As I started to swim away, he called after me. "Please tell me, striper: why are you seeking a better world? What's wrong with this one?"

I was loath to get into a long explanation. Yet there was something magnetic about this ugly old creature that drew me into his trust. So I told him how I'd lived with anger and boredom all the time I was in school.

"Perfectly understandable," he agreed. "You're like me. Not really an odd fish. Just too independent for such a highly structured life. Besides, in school you become so accustomed to following instructions, you lose your own instincts."

The two of us finally seemed to be hitting it off— "on the same wavelength," as we ocean inhabitants say. So I made the mistake of mentioning my coffee-colored stripes and the hurt and embarrassment they had caused.

"Ridiculous!" he exclaimed. "I spotted your stripes right away. They're striking."

I could hardly believe my ears. "Back in school," I explained, "my stripes became the bane of my existence."

The two lidless eyes of the octopus extended once again on their long protuberances for a closer examination. "In fact," he continued, "as I view them now, imprinted on your shiny silver scales, those coffee-colored stripes are simply stunning."

"But that's not what my schoolmates thought," I replied. "They considered me a freak."

"And is that how you see yourself?" countered the Old Philoctopus, boring in once again and squirting out another cloud of ink.

"I'm not sure," I said. "I've never seen my stripes."

"You mean you've never seen them with your two round fish eyes. That's not what I'm talking about. In your mind's eye, how do you visualize yourself? That's what matters."

Even though it was pitch black in the Andrea Doria's ballroom, I began to see the light. But before I could answer his question, he kept right on lecturing.

"See the scabby skin on my tentacles? You probably think it's ugly. I call it my royal coat of arms. It all depends on how you look at things. I see your colorful stripes as a badge of distinction, not disgrace. They set you apart."

I was so flustered I didn't know what to say. Though for a moment I wondered if the Old Philoctopus might be buttering me up before putting the squeeze on me with his scabby killer tentacles.

"The secret is to visualize yourself as the brave, intelligent, independent striped bass that you are," he continued. "Otherwise, you wouldn't have dared to venture way out here all alone."

I thought he'd never stop. But he finally ran out of steam, or maybe it was ink.

"Are you sure? Are you sure?" I kept repeating. "What you're saying isn't possible. You're not seeing the reality of my situation."

43

"All things are possible," proclaimed the Old Philoctopus, laboring hard once again to make what he was saying sink in. "It all depends how you look at them."

"But I'm a realist," I protested. "I try to see things as they are."

"So throughout your growing-up days," he interrupted, "the realist in you saw your coffee-colored stripes as the bars of a prison. They locked you in and kept you from being yourself. Isn't that the reality of your situation?"

I nodded my head in agreement.

"Well, now I'm setting you free. You must understand, reality is an illusion that can be overcome," he added, smiling—or what I assumed was a smile from the sideways movement of his ferocious beak.

All eight tentacles waved a friendly good-bye as I finally took my leave.

"One more thing," the wise Old Philoctopus called after me. "Remember, discovery is a quest. Perhaps you now will perceive the better world you were seeking. It isn't where you are that matters. It depends on what you do."

"Selecting another sinker, I clamped my teeth around the piece of lead."

Five

The moon rose high above the sea, painting the cresting waves pale silver. As I swam away from the Andrea Doria I felt free, liberated, like I'd never felt before. The Old Philoctopus had changed not only the direction I was headed but also the direction of my life.

"Solo," I said, "it's all right to go wild. Celebrate. No one's here to think you're showing off."

So I began by swimming mile-long sprints interspersed with soaring leaps into the air, following Carmen the porpoise's instructions. On each leap I aimed at the moon, trying to catch some of its shimmering light in my wide-open mouth before diving back into the sea.

How does a mouthful of moonlight taste? you might ask. Delicious! Try it sometime. It's subtle, but refreshing. Tickles the tongue like champagne. And it's healthy, too. Nourishes the soul without adding an ounce of fat.

"Solo, the Old Philoctopus was right," I said. "You've found the new world you were seeking. The wonder of it was always all around you. But you never relaxed enough to let the beauty seep in."

By morning, the moon, glowing a deep orange, slid down into the sea. "Time to take another mighty leap," I thought. "Better see what's ahead."

It's good that I did. A wild disturbance roiled the ocean's surface. At first glance it appeared to be caused by a series of underwater explosions. Eruptions of seaweed and spray were shooting into the air.

Better swim clear of that commotion, I decided. But then curiosity kept drawing me closer and closer until the sickening sight of countless bluefin tuna and swordfish, all hooked together, came into view. Most of them were half-dead, their eyes bulging from their heads, and their mouths opening and closing, desperately calling for help.

"How horrible!" Several tons of the most beautiful—and unfortunately for them, best-tasting—fish in the sea, were thrashing wildly without a chance to break free from the heavy monofilament line stretching for miles.

I asked myself, "Doesn't every living creature deserve the opportunity to fight for its own survival? Yes, even sharks, once given life, have the right to defend it."

"No use getting all worked up arguing with yourself, Solo. Every lamebrained fish in the world knows that longlines are the scourge of the ocean.

"Yet the biggest and most intelligent fish pounce on the bait, spaced out every thirty feet, as if it were being offered as some kind of free lunch. Even worse, you'd think by now they'd recognize the lights and radar reflectors fastened to these insidious rigs and give the longlines a wide berth."

For one terrifying moment I thought I spotted the blunt blue nose of Carmen caught on the line. I was about to bow my head in respect, when I saw it was a male porpoise, already dead.

I was still fuming, trying to figure out what could be done to outlaw these commercial fishermen and their longlines, when I took another flying leap and spied a fringe of green covering the horizon. Nantucket, I presumed. And only ten or fifteen miles away. But directly in my path a party boat bobbed up and down in the early-morning chop.

"Solo, what do you suppose they're fishing for? Blues, probably," I decided. "Possibly stripers, though I haven't seen any of my brethren hanging around. Certainly not weaks. Weakfish haven't shown up in these waters for years."

Ordinarily, I keep away from party boats. No point in tempting fate. But I was still trying to figure how to avenge the wholesale slaughter of those magnificent fish hooked on the longline, when I got to thinking:

"It isn't just commercial fishermen who deserve a comeuppance. The so-called sport fishermen also bait us. And in just as unfair ways. So why shouldn't we bait them back! I've often dreamed of doing that. But how?"

Approaching the party boat, I dove to the bottom, still uncertain

49

what I could do to get even with the guys at the other end of the dozen or so angling lines. But without getting hooked myself. As we stripers know, when it comes to matching wits with fishermen, they have the undisputed advantage.

As usual, each line had a sinker weighting it down. And tied some six inches above the sinker was a mouthwatering chunk of mackerel. Mouthwatering, that is, if you ignored the stainless-steel hook hidden inside.

Obviously, these party boat guys were all meat fishermen—bait-slingers, out to catch dinner, not really out for sport. Otherwise, they wouldn't be preying on our weakness for mackerel.

Eyeing all that bait, you'd never guess they had tackle boxes filled with even more tempting artificial lures: plugs gussied up with brightly colored feathers or wiggly rubber tails, and shiny silver spoons given such ridiculous names as Deadly Dicks and Swedish Pimples."

But then again, what would you expect? These party boat guys are born with silver spoons in their mouths. We die with them in ours. See, like I said: Right from day one, fishermen have the edge. Sometimes I think they might as well toss hand grenades into the sea and blow us all out of the water.

The party boat captain must have glanced at his fish finder and spotted the electronic blip that was me, because the chunks of mackerel began jigging up and down to catch my attention. All that did was make my stomach growl. Until suddenly the sight of the sinkers gave me a devilish idea.

50

"Solo," I thought, "here's your chance to level the playing field," if that expression applies to deep-sea fishing. But I must admit my initial anger had turned into a desire to do mischief.

At first I nibbled tentatively on one of the sinkers, making sure the baited hook remained a safe six inches above my head. Evidently the fisherman at the other end of the line missed the signal.

"He's either gabbing or guzzling beer," I figured. "Isn't that why they call them party boats?" So this time I grabbed his sinker with my mouth and gave it a good yank.

"Wow!" The response came instantly. Before I could spit out the piece of lead, it almost broke my teeth.

"Solo, you better be careful," I thought. "This little game could backfire badly."

Still, it was fun, picturing the frustrated fisherman when he furiously started reeling and his line went slack.

I decided to switch victims. Two frustrated fishermen, I decided, are better than one. They could commiserate with each other about the big one that got away.

Selecting another sinker, I clamped my teeth around the piece of lead and hung on for dear life, pretending to wage a pretty good fight. When I finally reached the surface and looked up, a phalanx of gawkers lined the party boat's rail. They were all jigging their rods like crazy, believing that a bunch of my schoolmates must be nearby.

"What a beauty!" I heard one of them exclaim. That sure puffed me up. And not a bleat about my coffee-colored stripes.

51

Then casually, as if I hadn't a worry in the world, I spit out the sinker and slipped back into the sea. A cascade of cussing followed me down to the bottom.

"Solo," I said, "this game is getting to be more and more fun. Now for the coup de grace—the ego-crushing blow that will keep any self-respecting fisherman from ever setting sail on a party boat again."

With still more mischief in mind, I carefully selected the biggest sinker I could cram into my mouth. Not a rough piece of lead like the previous two, but a polished chrome-plated diamond jig, so smooth it couldn't possibly catch in my teeth.

I'd barely grabbed it, when a pair of powerful arms began yanking me up to the boat.

"Turn, Solo! Turn!" I shouted to myself. "Point your head in the other direction."

I did. But as I veered away from the boat, the monofilament cut into my nose. Yet the joyful sensation of line ripping off the fisherman's reel dulled the pain.

Every time I gained a few feet, he quickly gained them back, until I my tail felt as heavy as an anchor.

I don't know how long the battle lasted, but it seemed eternal. I pretended I was the fish in The Old Man and the Sea. Although in that epic tale, Ernest Hemingway didn't describe the anguish of the fish. See, even in fiction, the fisherman gets first consideration.

Finally, with the line still stretched taut, I did an abrupt 180 and headed straight for the boat. Large loops of monofilament glistened in the water. "That sucker holding the rod figures he's lost me now." But it took only seconds before the slack was gone and I could see the shadow of the party boat's hull directly overhead.

"This is turning into a real test of nerves," I thought. "For me and for the fisherman."

So I darted under the boat until I felt the line chafing on the keel. "That'll scare him," I thought.

I guess it did. Right away, weaker pulls on the line indicated he'd loosened the drag on his reel, fearing that his twenty-pound test might fray.

I didn't want the line to break. That would spoil all the fun. So I reversed my field and doubled back under the keel to the fisherman's side of the boat.

Rays of blinding sunlight filtered down into the turquoise surface water, where I began swimming in smaller and smaller circles. I was certain the fisherman could see me now. His quivering graphite rod betrayed his excitement.

Leaping out of the water I saw the other fishermen, all pointing enviously at the prize their buddy was about to haul in.

The diamond jig was still clamped firmly between my teeth. But I kept shaking my head, faking an attempt to break free. "What a show you're putting on," I said to myself. "Now for the final act."

Feigning exhaustion, I rolled over onto my side and let the fisherman reel me right up to the boat. I heard loud cheers coming from the guys hugging the rail. "Way to go, Hank. You got him now!"

Hank, in his excitement, tried to lift all twenty-two pounds of me out of the water. Must be a novice, I figured, watching his rod curl into an upside-down U until the tip almost touched his reel.

"The net! Get the net!" I heard a voice shout as I opened my mouth and let the sinker fly out. The hook, with the mackerel still on it, almost smacked Hank in the face.

"Hey, Solo, turnabout's fair play," I said to myself. "You almost hooked a fisherman."

As gracefully as possible, I dove back into a wave. Not a clean Olympic-style dive, the kind I'd been practicing. But good enough to end the show.

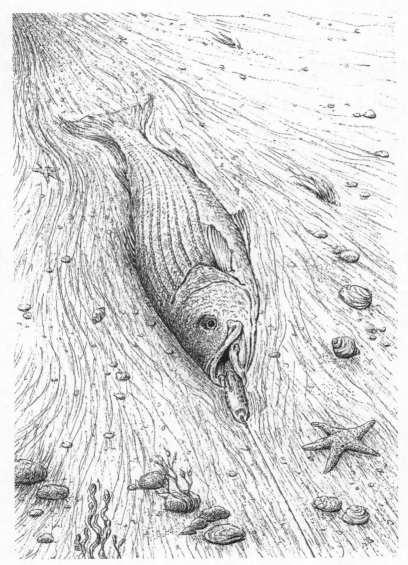

"With the plug sticking out of my mouth I dove for the bottom."

Six

This is about as close as I'll ever come to having paradise within my grasp. Crystal-clear water, white sand bottom with numerous kettle holes, and idyllic coves and lagoons to wander in and out of." That was my first reaction to the way Nantucket shows off its charms to a tourist striper.

I was too absorbed in my gorgeous new surroundings to chase after the local silversides. Or perhaps I was just too relaxed. "Wasn't that one of the Old Philoctopus's pronouncements? 'Relax and let the beauty sink in.' Although, the Old Philoctopus never said that was the secret of life. No, he never told me what the secret was."

Cruising through the narrow passage between Eel Point and tiny Tuckernuck Island at Nantucket's western tip, I spotted a pair of gray seals barking and frolicking near shore.

"Seals on Nantucket!" I marveled. Despite a few cold blasts blowing down from Canada, the weather was still warm. "Aren't you guys too far south for this time of year?" I felt like saying. But

I kept my big mouth shut. With seals, you never know if their bark's worse than their bite, or vise versa.

My sight-seeing was interrupted by a school of bunker thrashing convulsively in flight. A thousand silver tails began beating the sea around me into a white froth.

I've chased bunker myself, sometimes driving them right up onto the beach, where they died gasping for breath. So I sensed their terror. But I wondered what in the world they were they trying to escape from in such idyllic waters.

Then a rusty red bloom began spreading over the surface like an oil slick oozing from the ruptured hull of a tanker. "That's blood," I suddenly realized and quickly swam away to prevent it from coating my scales. "Poor fish! Their herd instinct made them so vulnerable."

Just beneath the surface, below the desperately thrashing bunker, I finally spotted a swarm of gluttonous blues biting, slashing, and chewing their bleeding victims into little pieces. I'd seen blues on a rampage before. But never such butchery. A pack of starving sharks couldn't have duplicated that mayhem.

With bulging stomachs, the sated blues slowly dispersed, the signal for a flock of herring gulls to swoop down, screeching and fighting for the leftovers before the outgoing tide swept them away.

"Who's next in that food chain?" I wondered. "Only ship-wrecked sailors eat seagulls."

All the commotion was so distracting I paid no attention to the lures being cast out in my direction. A group of surfcasters clustered on the beach must have noticed the diving gulls, a sign of fish in the vicinity. One after another, red, blue, green, and yellow plugs—but only faintly resembling minnows—plopped into the water close by. Finally, I realized it was me they were after.

"Do those stupid surfcasters really expect any self-respecting striper to strike at such shoddy imitations of a fish?" I wondered. "But then we stripers don't know if it's the gaudy colors or crazy shapes of artificial lures that catch the eye of fishermen, who shell out good money to buy them."

No use speculating on what motivates humans. They're too unpredictable. Especially fishermen. You never know in advance if they're kindhearted catch-and-release conservationists, or barbecuing connoisseurs who can't wait to slap you on their charcoal grill.

As must be obvious, my mind was on other things when a plump mackerel paraded by, wiggling its cute little tail and flaunting its mottled green and black markings. Without thinking, I pounced.

As I bit hungrily into its supposedly succulent rear end, all I could taste was paint and plastic. Then I felt a pinprick in the corner of my mouth.

"Oh no!" I heard a voice scream inside my head. "You're hooked!"

My first instinct was to flee toward the open sea as the bunker had been trying to do when the blues intercepted them. But straining against the taut line, I felt the barb dig deeper into

59

my jaw. Imagine the pain if a dentist drilled right through your tooth into your gum.

Unfortunately our protruding lower jaw makes it very difficult for us stripers to dislodge a plug. So I changed course and raced along parallel to the shore, furiously ripping line off the fisherman's reel. Through the pulsating monofilament, I could feel his defiance. This was no kindhearted catch-and-release conservationist. As clear as if it were coming through a telephone line, I heard his challenge:

"You and I, Mr. Striper, although temporarily tied together, are engaged in a deadly dual of endurance that only one of us can win."

I was ready. Like a boxer ducking a series of painful jabs, I began bobbing and weaving. All the practice jumps and speed-swimming exercises had prepared me for a fight. But against another fish. Not a human.

With the plug sticking out of my mouth like a fat cigar, I dove for the bottom. Perhaps by burrowing my nose in the sand and wiggling back and forth I could shake it loose.

What a stupid maneuver! Another hook dangling from the head of the plug caught my right gill. So I popped back up to the surface in even worse pain.

Regaining full speed, hoping to completely empty the fisherman's reel, I was seized by a better idea: Could one, or maybe two, wild jumps snap his tenuous twenty-pound test?

As I leaped from the water and hung acrobatically in the air, I saw the rod fly out of the fisherman's hands. "Quick, Solo," I said. "Drag that skinny pole of his out to sea, and victory is yours."

No such luck. The old boy reacted too fast. He reached down and plucked the rod from the boiling surf before the undertow took it away.

Splashing down again, I started zigging and zagging, desperately searching for a boulder to wrap the thin monofilament around. But the smooth sand bottom appeared to run on forever.

"Those lucky freshwater bass!" I thought. "They have an easier time winning their battles with so many underwater stumps to snag the line."

The monofilament was now pulled so taut it started to hum, strummed by the wind that was picking up. That might have been music to the fisherman's ears, but not to mine.

Suddenly the line went slack. I didn't feel it snap. I figured my razor-sharp pectorals had sliced it in two.

Visions of freedom flashed through my mind. "It's over! I'm loose! I'm outta here!" I exclaimed. At the same moment, I could almost hear the fisherman cursing the loss of his prize.

"No!" The barbed hooks just dug deeper into my gill and jaw, jolting me back to reality. My mouth was on fire and so was my brain.

Once again, I burst out of the water, standing on my tail and shaking my head, trying to throw the plug. The hooks rattled like castanets but didn't shake loose.

The sun was already hovering over the horizon, waiting to be extinguished by the sea. "Will I still be fighting this battle," I wondered, "when the moon peeks over the dunes?"

My worry now was about being caught in the curl of a wave and swept ashore. I could feel the fisherman pumping—slowly raising his rod tip until it pointed to the sky, and then quickly lowering it again to gain line. "Only rank amateurs do that," I thought. "It's a good way to bust the line."

On his next downstroke I lunged forward, hoping the sudden jolt would snap the monofilament. Instead, it flipped me over onto my side. Unable to right myself, I started spiraling in toward the beach.

My strength was ebbing. I wondered how many more leaps and lunges I could make. But even in my weakened state I still felt an exuberance for life that wouldn't let me die. Stripers, it's said, have a sinewed heart. Mine certainly wasn't ready to give out.

"And how do you feel, Mr. Fisherman?" I heard myself ask. "Are you finally wearing down?"

On my last leap I spotted him waist-deep in the surf, struggling to keep his balance. "Could I reverse the usual scenario," I wondered, "and drag him out to sea?"

What a crazy thought. I could just picture the poor soul, his waders filled with water, gasping for breath as he went under, still holding his rod aloft to keep the reel dry.

"Am I beginning to hallucinate?" I asked myself. "Did I really hear the staccato pop of the line snapping? Or is that my consciousness slipping away?"

I couldn't tell if I was sinking or floating. My whole body felt numb.

"Am I really going to die before I find out why I was given life? Am I going to end up stuffed and mounted on the wall of a tavern, listening to the barflies regale each other with fish stories?"

But then I supposed that was a nobler end for a striper than being eaten. A skilful taxidermist can bestow immortality on a fish, which is more than most fishermen can look forward to.

Tears blurred my eyes. "Or is the clear blue water turning inky black? Yes, Solo, you are dying!" I heard a hollow voice echo in my head. "You're dying. The Old Philoctopus was wrong. You finally have reached that place where the sky meets the sea. And without ever learning why you were put on this planet!"

"They're the Good-Cop-Bad-Cop duo," explained one of
  my escorts."

Seven

"C ould this be heaven?" I wondered. I had no memory of dying. Yet there I was, swimming through a sea of fleecy white clouds, escorted by a school of silver-winged flying fish.

"Where are we going?" I asked.

"To meet Gus," the flying fish sang out in unison.

"Who's Gus?" I cried, baffled by where I was and how I was able to swim through clouds with so little moisture to hold me up.

"The Great Universal Striper," they again answered as one. "He prefers to be called by his acronym, though some of us choose to address him more respectfully as Gus Almighty."

"Am I in heaven?" I finally blurted out.

But this time the flying fish didn't answer, because we had already reached a golden gate guarded by two gray seals. They looked faintly familiar. Then I vaguely recalled seeing a similar pair of seals on my tour of the Nantucket coast.

"And who might they be?" I asked, more mystified than ever. "I think I've seen them before."

"They're the Good-Cop-Bad-Cop duo," explained one of my escorts. "They guard Gus. Good Cop is the seal of approval.

Bad Cop, if you're not careful, will seal your fate. But don't get too close, because it's hard to tell one from the other."

"Presenting Solomon Starbucks Striper," barked the two seals in a raspy duet as I passed through the golden gate.

"They're announcing your arrival to Gus," explained one of the silver-winged flying fish.

Then I spotted the largest, most regal looking striper I'd ever seenñ-at least five feet tall from head to tail. His scales were of burnished gold, not silver, and his luminous stripes shined so brightly I thought they must be powered by an internal battery like an electric eel's.

"That's Gus," whispered my escort. "He's sizing you up."

I could feel the steely eyes of the Great Universal Striper boring right through me, though I must have passed muster.

"Welcome, Solomon," he said finally in a friendly voice that sounded as if he really was pleased to see me. "I've been waiting for you."

I lowered my head, the closest I could come to a bow. "Thank you, my lord," I murmured.

He grimaced at the salutation. "Please," he said, "just call me Gus." Then he launched into a lecture that seemed to go on forever."I summoned you, Solomon, because you keep questioning the purpose of your existence. Several times I heard you cry out, 'There must be more to life! More than just filling our stomachs and staying out of the stomachs of others.' Isn't that right, Solomon?"

I nodded my head, still too stunned to answer.

"Well, why do you think we gave you those distinctive coffee-colored stripes?" Gus continued. "It was to set you apart. To distinguish you from all your schoolmates. So you could lead them, and imbue in them your own courage and adventurous spirit. Wasn't that purpose enough? Do you understand what I'm saying, Solomon?"

Again I nodded, and bowed even deeper, as a sign of my rapt attention. Though at any moment I expected to fall out of the clouds and plunge back into the sea and reality.

Gus kept right on talking, never losing his friendly, fatherly tone. "You see, Solomon, I watched you teach yourself how to jump, and how to swim super-fast for long distances. Those were important accomplishments. I saw you look a killer shark in the eye and then defiantly race past his gaping jaws. I even admired the clever way you tricked those party boat fishermen, and the fierce fight you waged against the surfcaster on Nantucket. You made me proud, son."

I could see the flying fish fidgeting, impatient for Gus to finish. But he wasn't about to let me go.

"Yes, Solomon, you made me proud. Still, I was disappointed that you didn't go back and teach your schoolmates how to do those very same things. That was your responsibility, your personal mission. You owed it to your school, to your species, and to all future striper generations."

The flying fish all clapped their silver wings, to show their approval of the Great Universal Striper's message. "Speak up. Don't be afraid to answer," one of them whispered to me.

I felt befuddled, unsure what to say. Finally, the words just popped out of my mouth. "I'm confused, sir. I don't quite understand. I was an outcast, not a standout. My schoolmates ridiculed my coffee-colored stripes and forced me to swim at the tail end of the school. They would have laughed at any suggestions for self-improvement coming from me."

Gus just smiled. "I know," he said. "Your schoolmates, like most stripers today, are unconscionably conservative. They resist change. Even worse, they resent any striper who's different from them."

"So, sir, you knew of my humiliation," I replied, wondering why the all-powerful Great Universal Striper would have allowed such shabby treatment of one of his minions.

"Yes, Solomon. I didn't interfere. I wanted to test your character. It was part of my grand scheme."

I was beginning to get the picture, and it didn't please me one bit. "You mean my suffering was all preplanned?" I inquired, trying to conceal my irritation.

Calmly and patiently Gus expanded on what he had been trying to explain. "Let me put it this way, Solomon. Very little of what happens in this world is preordained, or preplanned as you say. But it is the obligation of every generation to acquire new knowledge and new skills. And then pass them on. Otherwise, we'd all be as backward as the Ice Age stripers were."

Gus's luminous stripes were now glowing brighter than ever. I also noticed what appeared to be a shimmering halo forming around his grizzled old head.

"But it takes a true adventurer, a daring innovator," he added, "a striper dissatisfied with the status quo, to bring all his brothers and sisters along. I'm still counting on you to make that your personal mission, Solomon. Because you are a one-in-a-million striper."

I felt my scales turning red, and I wondered if Gus could see me blushing with embarrassment. But I still wasn't satisfied with his explanation.

"Sir," I said, "you make the purpose of life sound so mundane. Were we put in the ocean only to improve our species? Is there no more mystery to life than that? No deep secret of our being?"

Before I could probe further, Gus flicked his tail to regain my attention.

"Yes, Solomon, but that secret can't be told. It defies explanation. It is one truth that can be known only by revelation."

I was still confused. Yet no more unsettled than I was by my strange surroundings.

"One more thing, Solomon. You can't continue through life as a loner. It's time to find a mate. That's another part of my grand scheme. The next striper generation needs thousands of little Solomons."

"But where will I find a compatible partner?" I asked. "All the females I've met resist change as much as the males."

"Follow your heart, Solomon. Follow your heart. That's another thing we've tried to instill in you. You may think of it as your ëother' compass. I heard you call it that. But just remember, almost always it will take you where you want to go."

Without warning, the Great Universal Striper disappeared, dissolving into the ether. And no sooner had he vanished than the fleecy white clouds changed into an angry thunderhead. The flying fish fled, leaving only the Good-Cop-Bad-Cop pair of seals to usher me out through the golden gate. I heard the gate slam shut as I suddenly lost my buoyancy and plummeted head-first into the void below.

**"Glancing back over my dorsal fin, there was the fat, old
schoolmaster."**

Eight

Floating on the surface, I was awakened by gentle waves lifting me up and lowering me down. Fingers of fading sunlight clawed at the darkening sky, and tinged the sea a rusty red.

"You're alive, Solo," I slowly realized. "Yes, you are alive!"

My mouth felt numb, though I could see the mottled green and black plug still hooked to my jaw. The pain was gone. But I continued slipping in and out of consciousness, barely aware of what had happened.

Finally, I looked back and saw the monofilament line trailing loosely in the water behind me.

"You're not only alive, Solo. You're free! You and that surf-caster are no longer connected."

As my mind began to clear, I dimly recalled the staccato pop of the line breaking just before I blacked out. Then everything became a dream, spiriting me away to that mystical place where the sky meets the sea, and from there, implausible as it seems, catapulting me up from the ocean into the clouds.

Crazy, isn't it, the tricks a delirious mind can play? So there's no point in my describing the godlike striper I met up there, who in some mysterious way still has me under his sway. Why else would I be smitten with the nagging desire to rejoin my former schoolmates, the same mean-spirited bunch that cast me out?

"Not so fast, Solo," I said to myself. "First you better unhook that fake mackerel from your mouth." If it weren't for the sharp barbs, its two hooks would have been easy to shake. They had already worn sizeable holes in my jaw and gill.

Diving to the bottom, I buried my head in the muck and wiggled back and forth, just as I tried doing during my battle with the surfcaster. But the hooks were still too deeply imbedded in flesh and bone to work loose.

I then swam around searching for a clump of seaweed. By plowing right through it, I hoped the big plug would get snagged and pull free. That didn't work either.

I was about to give up and live with that ugly green and black thing dangling from my mouth, when I heard a voice whisper, "Swim into the harbor, Solomon, and rub your head against a dock."

I wondered if I was still delirious. Then I vaguely recognized the fatherly tone from my dream.

"Is that you?" I called out, still not sure whether it was Almighty Gus or my imagination. But there was no answer. Waves lapping the shore were the only sound.

Not a bad idea, though. So I swam around Eel Point, and on past Dionis Beach, until I reached Nantucket Harbor. The ferry was just pulling away from Steamboat Wharf, so I could rub my head against the piles of the dock without fear of being crushed.

Nuzzling one of the heavy creosoted timbers, I succeeded in catching the plug's back hook in the rough wood. Then, whipping my tail from side to side, I shot ahead. But to the sickening sound of tearing flesh.

Warm blood oozing from inside of my mouth trickled down my throat. If a fisherman ever endured such excruciating pain he'd file down the barbs on his hooks and give us stripers a sporting chance.

Suddenly, the rear hook broke loose from the pile. "Solo," I said, "no use worrying about some callous, uncaring fisherman. You've got your own problem to solve."

So once again I rubbed my head against the rough wooden pile until the rear hook caught hold. But on each attempt to move forward and pry the plug loose, I tasted more blood. "Careful, Solo," I warned myself, "or you'll bleed to death."

There didn't seem to be any solution when the wake of a passing powerboat slapped me hard against the dock, ripping both hooks right out of my head.

"Well done," whispered the voice, as I glanced back at the green and black lure hanging from the pile, just waiting for some surprised fisherman to pick up and stick in his tackle box.

"Are you still watching over me, Gus?" I asked. If he answered, his voice was drowned out by a blast from the ferryboat whistle. Whether it was Gus's influence or not, I felt an overwhelming desire to take my sore mouth back to the coast and look for my old school.

With my recently acquired speed, I was able to cover the distance between Nantucket and Cape Cod in less than an hour.

"Now where?" I wondered. "Locating a single striper school between the Cape and Chesapeake Bay could take forever."

"Follow your heart, Solomon," whispered the voice. "Follow your heart. As I explained before, it will take you where you want to go."

"Gus, you're beginning to spook me with all that whispering," I replied. But again there was no answer.

Following my heart was easy. It was already set on swimming to Montauk Point on the eastern tip of Long Island. "Plenty of sand eels there," I thought. "Easy pickings while my sore mouth heals."

In two more hours of speed swimming, I recognized the powerful beam from Montauk Light penetrating the choppy night sea.

"At last, Solo, you're back in familiar waters," I rejoiced. "Far from the Old Philoctopus, and Carmen the porpoise, and the Good-Cop-Bad-Cop pair of seals. Yes, and far from Almighty Gus, the Great Universal Striper, although he seems to be everywhere you go."

I was still celebrating, when a voice, not Gus's, beckoned from behind: "Welcome home, Solomon Starbucks Striper. We heard you were coming."

76

Glancing back over my dorsal fin, there was the fat, old schoolmaster. The one who had ridiculed my coffee-colored stripes, and then bawled me out for not blending in.

"You mean you expected me?" I replied, stunned by both his sudden appearance and friendly voice.

"What goes around comes around," he said, using one of his tired clichés that I remembered so well. "But we weren't sure. The tidal telegraph's no more reliable than the jungle telegraph or grapevine on shore."

The schoolmaster's warm reception, I must admit, made me feel good. But I was still suspicious. "What about my school-mates?" I asked. "They hate the color of my stripes."

"They're excited," said the schoolmaster. "They've heard about your exploits. They, too, want to learn how to jump and swim at high speeds, and use their compasses to guide them on journeys far out to sea."

Was this sweet talk? I wondered. Simply a trick to woo back an outcast? "But all my schoolmates ever cared about was filling their stomachs," I said. "They didn't want to learn anything new."

Clearly, the conversation wasn't going well. Then Gus interceded. "Don't be so hard-nosed, Solomon," he whispered. "Be more trusting and forgiving."

I felt like telling Gus to bug off. But that wouldn't have been respectful. Anyway, before I could say another word, the entire school had formed a circle around the schoolmaster and me.

"We want Solo. We want Solo," they chanted. "We want you to be our leader."

I could see the old schoolmaster grimacing. Obviously, this wasn't music to his ears. But he couldn't ignore the pleadings of all his followers. "You see," he said, pointing at me. "You've been chosen by acclamation."

The next day we began classes. I swam side by side with my former schoolmates, guiding and pressuring them through rough and smooth seas. They liked the practice because it was fast and exciting. By nightfall they were exhausted. But their hunger, once directed only at finding more food, was now concentrated on learning.

I must admit it was easier teaching these eager stripers the hydrodynamics of jumping and the mechanics of speed swimming than it was ridding them of what I called their IAs—the inhibiting assumptions that had been drummed into them since birth.

"Forget all those old constraints," I kept saying. "Break the chains of your thought, and you break the chains of your body."

Fortunately, they were quick studies. When I said, "Shorten your tail strokes and start using your pectorals," they immediately caught on. And when I explained the energy-conserving principle of power gliding with the tide, another one of Carmen's concepts, they soon got the hang of that too. But the power of visualization, as preached to me by the Old Philoctopus, they found hard to grasp.

"In your mind's eye," I kept repeating, "you must see yourself jumping before you can jump very high. You must picture yourself swimming fast to really gain speed."

At first my words seemed to dissolve unheeded in the sea. It took a few weeks of swimming together in tight formation for my students to understand the importance of visualization, and absorb it into their very being.

Finally they did, and the entire school was able to cover the fourteen nautical miles between Montauk Point and Block Island in just half an hour. That is, all except the old schoolmaster, who admitted being stuck in his ways and stayed behind at Montauk filling his gut.

The jumping lessons went like gangbusters too, although at first a few nonbelievers told me to face reality, reciting the old refrain "Bass can't jump."

"Remember, friends, reality is simply an illusion that can be overcome," I explained, once again quoting the Old Philoctopus. In a few more weeks, one after another, my charges were flying out of the water and standing on their tails, pretending they were tarpon performing an aquatic dance.

Surprisingly, all during these lessons not a word was uttered about my coffee-colored stripes. Once in a while when I pushed too hard, a couple of the students would cry out, "Hey, King Solomon, who do you think we are?"

Without fail, I'd rise to the bait. "The bible may describe King Solomon's power over fish," I'd protest. "But I'm just an ordinary striper who's mastered a few new skills."

"Just kidding," they'd shout. "Just kidding. We love you, Solo."

Even more surprising was my affection for them. Several times I asked myself, "How could you love the same stripers who hated your guts and cast you out? It defies all logic."

Suddenly it occurred to me that if they hadn't forced me to leave, I wouldn't have been challenged to chase my dreams and master these important new skills. Besides, I would have missed all the adventures that made my life so exciting.

Once again I heard that familiar whisper, though this time I wasn't sure if it was Gus Almighty, or a voice coming from inside my head: "At last you followed your heart, Solomon Starbucks Striper. At last you followed your heart.

"And see, it didn't lead you astray. Instead it led you back to your brothers and sisters. And without detracting one iota from your adventurous spirit. You are still the same stubbornly independent striper you always were. Except now I believe you've discovered the secret of life. And it wasn't such a mystery after all."

"Is that you, Gus?" I asked, expecting only silence. "Why don't you ever answer?"

To my surprise, the voice continued, "See, you never stopped pursuing your dreams. That is the secret of life, although deep down you knew it all the time.

"What you didn't understand was that dreams are like the ocean's tides. They sweep you along to places and possibilities you couldn't even imagine. And when the dreams fade and the

80

tides turn, they carry you back to where you began. But the wondrous experiences encountered along the way remain part of you forever."

"On most of his travels he was accompanied by Sylvia Starbucks Striper."

Epilogue

For the next fifteen years, Solomon Starbucks Striper kept on switching schools, all the while teaching members of his species how to jump high above the waves like a tarpon and streak through the sea with the speed of a porpoise.

At the same time, he challenged his students to make long journeys of exploration, relying on their infallible internal compasses to deliver them to their desired destinations—and then guide them safely home. But before his students could accomplish these feats, he had to rid them of the inhibitions, which ever since the Ice Age have kept all stripers from venturing far out to sea.

On most of his travels he was accompanied by Sylvia Starbucks Striper, an attractive she-bass he met at Shagwon Reef near Montauk Point. It was love at first sight. Sylvia admitted being infatuated with his coffee-colored stripes and quickly took his name, although her stripes were as black as coal.

Every fall they returned together to the Nanticoke River, swimming up from lower Chesapeake Bay, past Roaring Point and Vienna, to their freshwater coupling bed in Big Creek Marsh.

There, while bumping heads in the traditional mating dance dubbed "rock fights" by local fishermen, pale ribbons of pearly eggs poured from Sylvia's bulging belly. Over them, he cast jets of fertilizing sperm. But not one of their fry developed coffee-colored stripes.

On what turned out to be his last journey south, he told Sylvia to swim on ahead to the Chesapeake. He would rejoin her there. The sea was still warm and soothing to his tired old body. Warm enough, anyway, for him to hang around Block Island, his favorite feeding ground.

For days he chased sand eels and silversides in and out of Great Salt Pond, the island's spacious bait-filled harbor, preparing for his long winter fast. His days of dreaming were over. Or at least his dreams had dimmed. His main interest now was filling his stomach, as was the case when he was young.

Down at the south end of the island, he poked around Black Rock and the other giant boulders, which, hidden at high tide, had torn gaping holes in the hulls of many ships and left them rusting on the bottom. The sunken wrecks sheltered great quantities of mussels and crabs, which he considered a great delicacy.

The sun's fireball was about to slip into Block Island Sound late one afternoon, when he spotted a juicy, foot-long eel meandering along the bottom. It was such an easy mark, he was almost ashamed to grab it. But in a couple of gulps he swallowed the thing whole. Only then did he suddenly feel the piercing pain of a steel hook caught in the wall of his stomach.

Joe Szabo, who earned his living chasing swordfish and giant tuna far out in the Atlantic Canyon, never stopped dreaming of the day he would catch a magnificent, record-size striper back home on Block Island. Earlier that afternoon he had picked up a couple of live eels at the Twin Maples bait shop and drove out to his favorite surfcasting spot at Southwest Point.

"The sky was clear," he recalls, "but horrendous waves crashing against the boulders drenched me with spray."

He spent a fruitless hour casting and retrieving his eels, until there was just a glimmer of life left in any of them. Still, he treasured the solitude and kept on casting, ignoring the sting of the salt spray hitting his face.

As the sun sat on the horizon, ready to dip into Block Island Sound, Joe felt a heavy tug.

"The big bass hardly fought at all," he said. "He picked up my eel and practically ran up onto the beach with it. I guess he was too old and tired to give me much of a tussle."

That, of course, was a pallid tale to tell after bringing home a monster striper that tipped the scales at seventy and one-half pounds, setting a Rhode Island record. But as so often happens with fish stories, it was embellished bit by bit by the island residents, many of who had also fantasized for years about catching such a magnificent fish while casting from the shore. To hear them tell it, Joe was almost dragged out to sea in a marathon battle that lasted from dusk to dawn.

Today, Solomon Starbucks Striper hangs on the wall of Rebecca's Takeout Restaurant, run by Joe's wife. If you visit Block Island, stop by and admire this trophy striper that appears so lifelike you'll think it's about to leap off the wall.

On closer inspection, however, you can tell that the taxidermist was perplexed by its strange coffee-colored stripes. They've been brushed over lightly with a coat of black paint.